For Jack and Jackson
—L. A.

To all the children and all they know
—J.D.

All We Know
Text copyright © 2016 by Linda Ashman
Illustrations copyright © 2016 by Jane Dyer
All rights reserved. Manufactured in China.
No part of this book may be used or reproduced in any manner whatsoever
without written permission except in the case of brief quotations embodied in critical
articles and reviews. For information address HarperCollins Children's Books,
a division of HarperCollins Publishers, 195 Broadway, New York, NY 10007.
www.harpercollinschildrens.com

Library of Congress Control Number: 2014952534
ISBN 978-0-06-168958-1

The artist used watercolor, Dr. Ph. Martin's acrylic, and pencil on American
M. Graham & Co. artists' gouache on Arches 140 lb. hot press paper.
Typography by Rachel Zegar
15 16 17 18 19 SCP 10 9 8 7 6 5 4 3 2 1
❖
First Edition

ALL WE KNOW

By Linda Ashman   Illustrated by Jane Dyer

HARPER
An Imprint of HarperCollinsPublishers

A cloud knows how to rain.

The thunder, how to boom.

A bulb knows when it's time to sleep

and when it's
time to bloom.

A seed knows how to sprout.

A lamb knows how to bleat.

A bee knows where the nectar is

to make the honey sweet.

The fox knows how to make a home
inside a cozy log.

And no one taught the tadpole
how to be a frog.

A crab knows how to crawl.

A seagull, how to soar.

A wave knows how
to rise up tall

and tumble to the shore.

A squirrel can leap
from tree to tree.

A mole can dig a hole.

And beans don't need a lesson
in how to climb a pole.

A pup knows how to wag.

A kitten, how to play.

Swallows fly to winter homes
and never lose their way.

The oak knows when to
sprout new leaves—

and when to let them go.

The pumpkin knows
exactly how

to grow ...   and grow ...

and grow.

A bear knows when to wander
and when it's time to doze.

The hare knows when
it's best to wear
its whiter winter clothes.

The stars know how to shine.
The earth knows how to turn.

The sun knows when to wake each day—
it didn't need to learn.

And—not so very long ago,
on a moonlit night—

you knew how to tell me
that the time was finally right.

The days know how to march along
no matter what we do.

And I know how to love you.
No one taught me . . .

I just knew.